# Lily the Bear's Big Event

written and illustrated by Cindy S. Terry

To Amy,
My lily pal!
Remembering
those "den days"
forever,
for the love of bears
Cindy S Terry
2010

A very special thank you to the Wildlife Research Institute, the North American Bear Center, and to the people who work and volunteer there and love bears. To Dr. Lynn Rogers and Sue Mansfield, a heartfelt thanks for the amazing research that you do. I am grateful that you put this event on the internet to be shared with all.

Lily the Bear's Big Event
Copyright © 2010 by Cindy S. Terry
Published by Blackberry Ridge Publishing,
a subsidiary of Blackberry Ridge Designs
West Liberty, Ohio
All rights reserved. No part of this book may be reproduced or transmitted
in any form or by any means without written permission from the author.

The references to Dr. Lynn Rogers and his work have been used with permission.

ISBN 978-0-578-06259-4

Printed and bound in Canada

To order additional copies of this book please go to www.lilythebearsbigevent.com

For Laurel,

*For Laurel,*
*perhaps more education would have saved you.*

*For James,*
*my treasured husband of 36 years, who shares with me the love of*
*all of God's wonderful creation!*

"I feel so alone today," Lily said to herself.  A pinecone fell from a tall tree and bounced off a rock near her den.  She peeked out to see what it was, but all she could see were the colorful trees in the big forest around her.  Then she looked up.  "Oh, look at you!" Lily said.  A little black and white nuthatch landed on the branch above Lily's den.  "I guess I'm not alone after all," she said to the bird.

Lily felt something walking up her back, down her arm, and then right off her paw.  "Now, what was that?"  She looked down.  A tiny brown mouse with a little white mustache looked up at her, smiling.  "Hi, my name is Speedy," said the mouse.  "Hello Speedy, I'm Lily the bear," she replied. "Why are you in my den?"  "Why indeed," the little mouse responded, "because I'm getting ready for winter and I don't want to miss the big event!  I am sorry I walked on you."

"Oh, it just tickled a bit," giggled Lily. "That's because of this old cane I walk with." Speedy smiled as he held up a tiny twig. "I used to be able to run super fast. That's why my friends call me Speedy." His smile faded to a frown. "Unfortunately my 'speedy' days are over.

I must go now,
and get ready for winter.
It will take a while."

He started to walk off,
and then he turned back to Lily
and asked,

"Do you mind sharing your den?
I thought I might stay
and watch the big event."

"Oh, I don't mind," said Lily. Speedy walked off as fast as an old mouse with a cane could walk. "But what big event is Speedy talking about?" Lily thought to herself.

"Hello, black bear," A soft voice came from inside the den.   Lily scratched her head and looked all over.  Then, she looked again.  Finally, she saw a very, very tiny spider, hanging from a thin strand of web, and looking straight at her. "Oh there you are!" said Lily in surprise. "Who are you?" she asked.   "My name is Charlotte" said the tiny spider.  Lily twitched her big black ears.  "Hello Charlotte.  Why are you in my den?" asked Lily. "I don't want to miss the big event, that's why!"

"I was wondering if I could hang around here for the winter." She climbed a little bit higher. "Oh, that would be fine." said Lily, "There is a mouse staying here too."

"I know," said Charlotte. "His name is Speedy. He is an old friend of mine." Charlotte climbed behind a rock. "Please don't go yet," said Lily, "I need to ask you…" The spider was gone. "Well, this is an exciting day! I am not alone after all!"

Speedy and Charlotte came back before lunchtime.  "Did you see?  It started to snow!" Lily shouted.

"Hushhh …" said Speedy, "I hear someone walking in the forest."  Lily sniffed the air.  "Maybe Dr. Lynn is coming!"  She said to her two new friends.  "Don't be afraid, Dr. Lynn is very nice."  Charlotte climbed up the den wall until she was hidden in the shadows.  "Who is Dr. Lynn?" she whispered.

"Dr. Lynn watches over all the bears in the forest," Lily said. "He always brings me grapes and talks to me.  Last summer, I even let him put this collar on me."

"I was wondering what that was." said Speedy.  He pointed at Lily's collar with his cane. "Dr. Lynn said that this collar means I'm a special bear!"  Lily said this with her nose in the air. "Oh sure," said Speedy, rolling his eyes.  He slowly climbed out of the den and stood on top. He looked out into the woods.

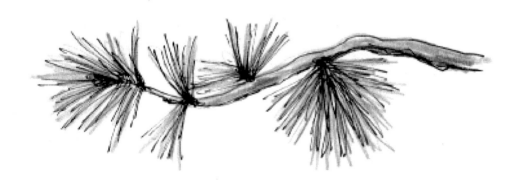

"Attention everyone!  Dr. Lynn is in the forest!"  Speedy announced loudly from the top of the den.  "He is carrying a long white tube."   "What is a long white tube for?"  Charlotte wondered.  "Well, I want to meet him now that I know he is so nice."

"It's me bear," Dr. Lynn said as he walked closer. "Don't be afraid, Lily" he said in the calm voice he always used.  Dr. Lynn knew a lot about bears and he was always careful.  He laid down the long white tube he was carrying.

"What are you doing?" Lily asked Dr. Lynn as she climbed out of the den.  Charlotte crept up the rock next to Speedy, so she could see.  "I'm putting this tube close to your den." Dr. Lynn said.  "Inside the tube is a special camera. With this camera, thousands and thousands of people will be able to watch you.  They will go on the internet and see right into your den! Now everyone can watch the big event!"   "Yeaaaa!" cheered Speedy and Charlotte as they jumped up and down.  "Everyone will get to see the big event!"   But Lily just scratched her head and wondered what they were talking about.

Dr. Lynn took a long time tying the white tube to a tree. "There now, nice and tight. It should not move. Good bye everyone," he said as he left the forest. Lily, Speedy, and Charlotte watched as he walked far, far away.

"Why does everyone know about the big event, except for me?" asked Lily. But no one was there to answer her. Her new friends had gone into the woods to look for lunch. "I don't feel too hungry today. I'm just very tired." Lily thought. She stretched and sniffed the air sensing it was almost time to hibernate.

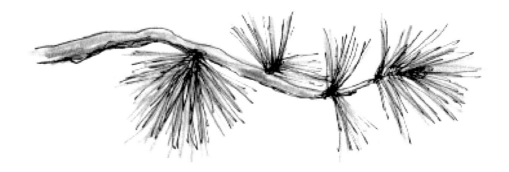

That evening, the three new friends cuddled together in Lily's den. "Lily, you sure have nice warm fur!" Charlotte said as she climbed into the soft fur. "I will sleep behind this rock," Speedy decided. Lily yawned. "I am so tired! But I can't sleep. I keep thinking about that white tube. I don't understand...what is …the big event…?" "Go to sleep," Charlotte whispered, "Speedy and I are here."

Lily slept for almost two months, she even missed Christmas.

"Charlotte, where are you?" called Speedy one cold morning. "I can't find my cane. It might be under Lily, and I don't want to wake her up." Charlotte stretched her eight tiny legs and yawned. "I will help you look. Why do you need your cane now anyway?" "I need to go into the forest and look for breakfast," he said rubbing his belly. Charlotte thought about this. "It is sure a good thing that Lily doesn't need to eat. How do bears go so long without eating?"

"Oh look! I found your cane!" shouted Charlotte. "Right here under Lily's paws." "What would I ever do without you, little spider?" said Speedy. Then, he walked through the snow, to find some seeds he had hidden under a log. While Charlotte watched Speedy, she saw Lily roll over and yawn.

"Lily is not sleeping very well." Charlotte said to Speedy when he returned. "She has been tossing and turning for hours!" He put his fresh supply of seeds neatly in the corner of the den. "Maybe it is almost time for the big event." "Oh, I hope so. I can't wait!" they whispered together.

"What time is it?" Lily grunted. "Go back to sleep. It's the middle of January," said Speedy. "I can't sleep. I don't feel good!" Lily growled. "I know what we can do. We will sing you a song!" Charlotte decided. Speedy looked at her with a frown. "We will? But I don't like to sing!" "Well," said Charlotte with a smile, "singing always makes me feel better." She began to sing a sweet song her mom used to sing to her. Speedy sang too, even though he didn't know the words. Lily tossed and turned. "That is a nice song, but it's not making me feel any better." Speedy didn't know what to do. "I will go outside and look for Dr. Lynn," he decided.

Speedy left as fast as he could. "Oh, my," cried Lily, "Why can't I get comfortable?" She slammed her body against the side of the den. Charlotte stopped singing and climbed to a safer place.

# What are you doing in there?

......Speedy shouted. "I think it is time for the cub to be born!" Charlotte shouted back to Speedy. "Cub?" asked Lily, "Am I going to have a baby? Is this the big event? Why, of course it is!" Lily thought to herself. "It all makes sense now! It is the middle of January. It is time for black bears, like me, to have their babies! It's time..... NOW!"

"What's happening?" cried Speedy. "I want to see! I want to see!" All that Speedy could see was Lily's black furry back.

Underneath Lily, lying in the soft bed of leaves was her new baby bear!  The little cub reached out and touched Lily's nose with her tiny paw.  "Mmmh, mmmh, mmmh." grunted Lily, making mama bear sounds.  The baby started to cry.

"It sounds just like a human baby crying!" said Charlotte.  "It's OK baby bear," Lily said softly to her cub.  "Don't cry."  Then she blew a huge breath of warm air onto the cub.  "Now the baby will be warm."  Speedy had managed to climb around Lily and get into the den.

"I want to see the new baby!  Oh, Lily, what a sweet baby cub you have.  It is so sad that Dr. Lynn isn't here.  I'm sure that he would like to see your cub too!" Speedy said as he watched the new little baby.  He and Charlotte had forgotten all about the white tube tied to the tree just outside the den.  The camera inside the tube was taking live video pictures while people watched on the internet.  With this camera, all the people could see right into Lily's den. Even though they were not in the woods with Lily, they could all watch her baby being born.

"Hussshh, listen!  Do you hear the baby cub making sounds?"  Charlotte asked him. "Yes, I hear those noises.  It sounds like a motor running!"  Speedy said.  "Uhu, uhu, uhu,…. uhu, uhu, uhu," hummed the little cub.  "That's funny!"  Charlotte laughed.
 "All baby bears make that noise when they are drinking milk from their mama's."  Lily explained.  Speedy and Charlotte smiled.  They were so happy.  Charlotte started to sing the song that she had taught them.  This time Speedy sang too.

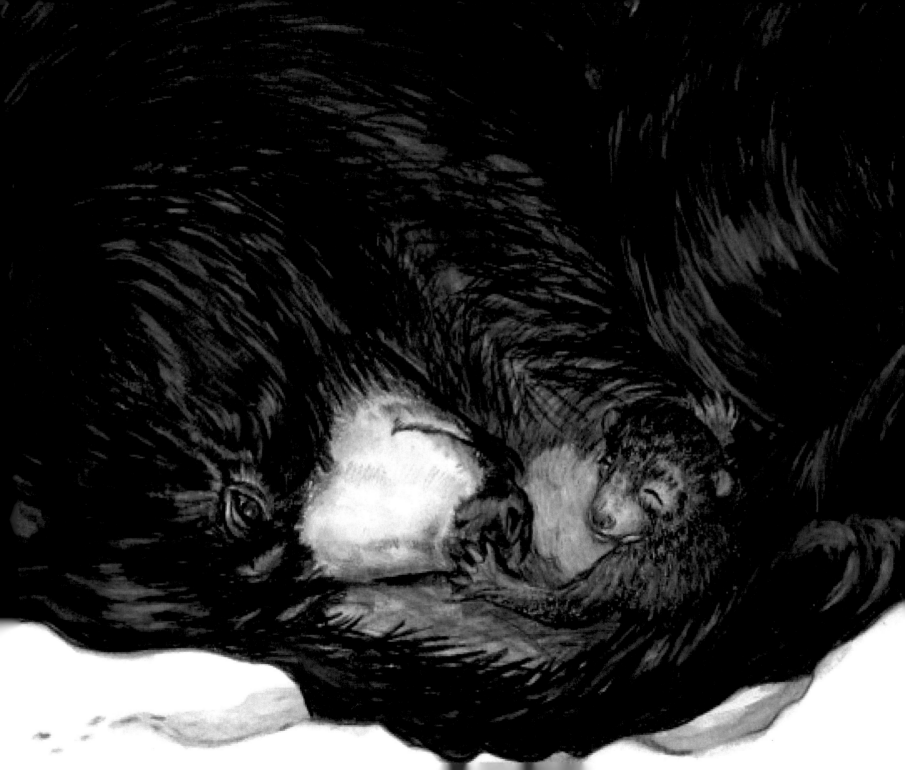

"I think the baby is asleep now," whispered Lily. "I'm going to lay here and decide what to name my new little cub." "Oh yes, the baby needs a name." Speedy nodded. Charlotte yawned. "Well. I'm too tired to think right now. I'm going to climb down into Lily's fur and take a nap." "Good idea!" Speedy said, "You will be snug as a cub in a mama bears hug!" "Oh, Speedy! You always make me laugh." Charlotte said grinning.

All of the people watching on the internet started grinning too! They could see inside the den because of the special camera in the long white tube. They could hear the baby cub cry. They could watch her take a nap. And do you know what? The people watching on the internet even helped Lily think of a name for her baby. So you see, Lily and her cub, and Speedy, and Charlotte, were never alone at all!

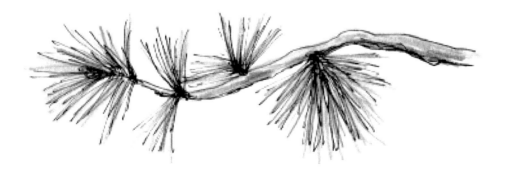

Do you want to know what Lily named her baby?
Would you like to know more about black bears?   You can go on the internet to:

# www.bear.org

This is the site for the North American Bear Center in Ely, Minnesota.  Lily and her cub live in the wild woods, near Ely.  They help the research of Dr. Lynn Rogers and the bear center and have brought joy and education into many peoples' lives.

Please remember to respect wildlife and never approach or feed a wild bear.

*Authors Note*

This story is based on true events. Lily the Bear is a wild black bear living in the north woods near Ely, MN. Dr. Lynn Rogers installed a live streaming camera just outside Lily's winter den after gaining her trust. The researchers were hoping she would have cubs in January, and Lily had her first cub on Jan. 22, 2010. Tens of thousands witnessed the event, thousands of troops watched overseas, and hundreds of children watched in classrooms. Talk shows, newspapers, and broadcasts all covered this history making moment. Lily has a dedicated following of over 95,000 Facebook friends. She has captivated the hearts of many, including mine.